For David

Scholastic Children's Books,
Commonwealth House, 1-19 New Oxford Street,
London WC1A 1NU, UK
a division of Scholastic Ltd

London – New York – Toronto – Sydney – Auckland
Mexico City – New Delhi – Hong Kong

First published in hardback by Scholastic Ltd, 1999
This paperback edition published by Scholastic Ltd, 2002

Text and illustrations copyright © Sue Heap, 1999

ISBN 0 439 99874 3

Printed and bound in China
All rights reserved

2 4 6 8 10 9 7 5 3 1

Princess Dress

Sue Heap

Hippo

The sun rose up on Pasta Palace.

Inside Pasta Palace, Princess Dress woke up. She was very excited because today was her birthday.

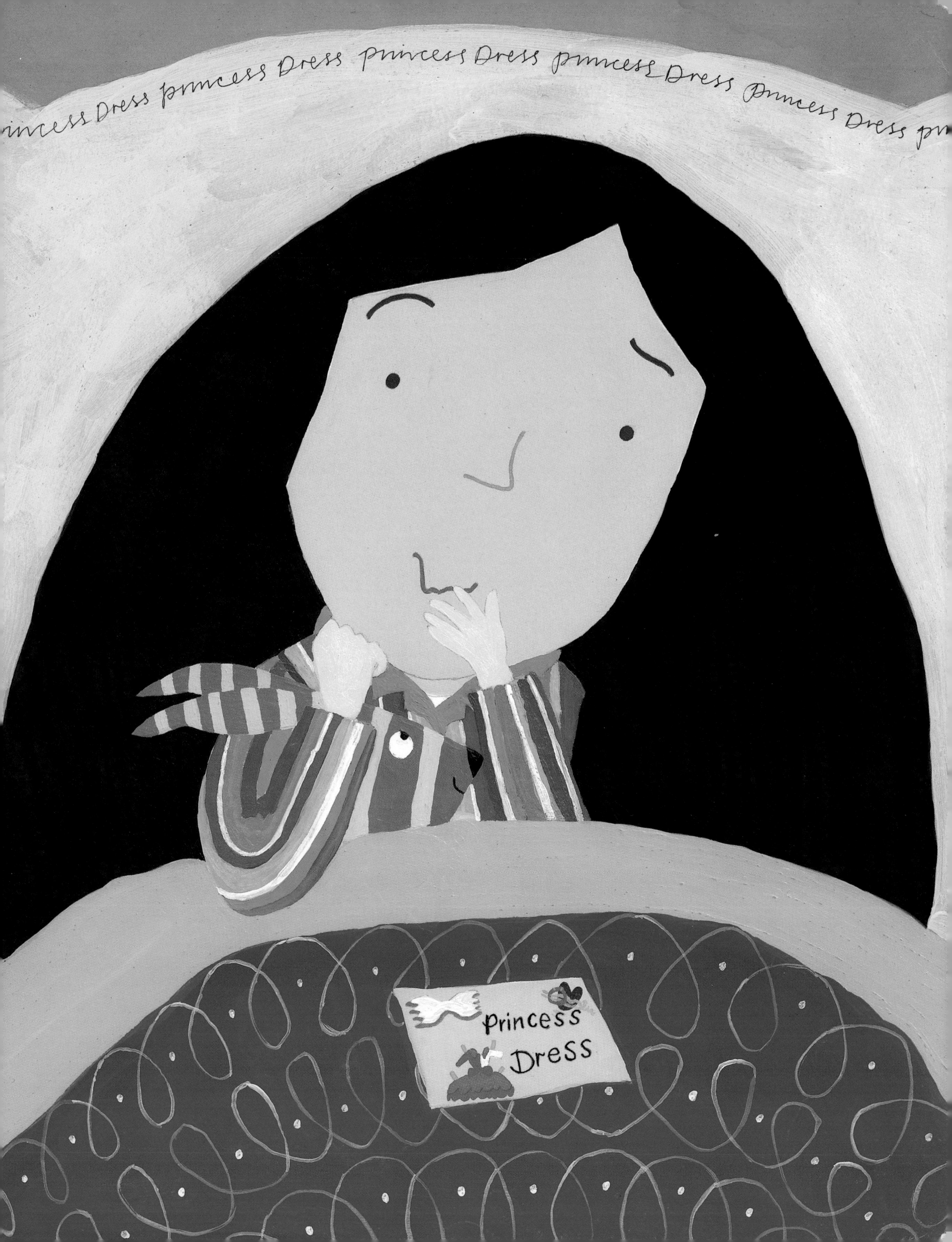

She wondered which dress to wear to her party.

She called for her seven servants and
seven best dresses.

She liked her red dress
but it was too itchy and hot!

She loved the orange dress
she'd worn last year, but now
it was just too small!

She wasn't sure about her yellow dress
because it was too fussy!

She didn't like
her green dress,
it was too plain!